Clam Digging

with Grandma

The Nunavummi reading series is a Nunavut-developed levelled book series that supports literacy development while teaching readers about the people, traditions, and environment of the Canadian Arctic.

Published in Canada by Nunavummi, an imprint of Inhabit Education Books Inc. | www.inhabiteducation.com

Inhabit Education Books Inc.
(Iqaluit) P.O. Box 2129, Iqaluit, Nunavut, X0A 1H0
(Toronto) 191 Eglinton Avenue East, Suite 301, Toronto, Ontario, M4P 1K1

Design and layout copyright © 2019 Inhabit Education Books Inc.
Text copyright © Inhabit Education Books Inc.
Illustrations by Tamara Campeau © Inhabit Education Books Inc.

Printed in Canada.

Library and Archives Canada Cataloguing in Publication

Title: Clam digging with Grandma / written by Hannah Gifford ; illustrated by Tamara Campeau.
Names: Gifford, Hannah, 1984- author. | Campeau, Tamara, illustrator.
Description: Series statement: Nunavummi reading series
Identifiers: Canadiana 2019019362X | ISBN 9780228702818 (hardcover)
Classification: LCC PS8613.I328 C53 2020 | DDC jC813/.6—dc23

ISBN: 978-0-2287-0281-8

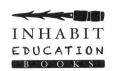

INHABIT
EDUCATION
BOOKS

Clam Digging
with Grandma

WRITTEN BY
Hannah Gifford

ILLUSTRATED BY
Tamara Campeau

Silu is excited to spend the weekend at her grandma's house. Her dad told her the tides would be low, so they can all go clam digging! Silu has never been clam digging before.

On Saturday morning, Silu and her grandma get ready to go clam digging.

"*Anaanatsiaq*,* what do we need to bring?" asks Silu.

"We'll need garden spades, a bucket, rubber gloves, and rubber boots," says Grandma.

Silu starts packing their supplies.

*anaanatsiaq (pronounced "a-NAA-nat-si-aq"): grandmother

"We should also pack a lunch. I made some bannock and caribou stew," says Grandma.

"*Niam!*"* says Silu.

Grandma says it might be cold and rainy, so they wear clothes that will keep them warm and dry. Soon they are ready to go.

*niam (pronounced "NI-am"): yummy

When Silu and Grandma arrive at the shoreline, Silu's dad is waiting at the boat. Silu waves at him excitedly. She can't wait to go clam digging!

They climb onto the boat and load their supplies.

When they get on the boat, Silu asks, "How far are we going?"

"Our favourite spot is about 30 minutes away. It is the best place for clam digging," says Grandma.

When they arrive at the spot, they see a lot of other people and boats there.

"Are they clam digging, too?" asks Silu.

"Yes. I told you it was a good spot!" says Grandma. "It's very sandy here, so there are lots of clams."

They get off the boat and start walking on the wet sand.

"Look for little holes in the sand," says Grandma. "The clams stick their necks out from the holes. If you step near them, they might squirt water at you!"

Silu starts looking for holes in the sand. All of a sudden, a stream of water squirts out from one of the holes by her feet! She looks down and sees a little neck poking out of the hole.

"Look, I see one!" says Silu.

Grandma shows Silu how to dig out the clam.

"Grab the shell and hold very tight," says Grandma. Silu grabs the shell of the clam and holds it as tightly as she can.

"As you're holding the shell, dig in the sand around the clam," says Grandma. "But be quick, because the clam will start to burrow!"

Silu digs as quickly as she can. Then the clam comes loose. She has her first clam!

Silu looks proudly at her clam.

"Good job!" says Grandma. Silu places her clam in the bucket.

They keep walking and collecting clams. Along the way, they see all kinds of creatures. They see a baby sculpin, a starfish, seashells, and a little jellyfish.

After a while, they have almost filled a whole bucket with clams!

"The tide is rolling in," says Grandma. "That means it's time for lunch."

They go up to the land to eat their caribou stew and bannock.

After lunch, Dad takes them back to Grandma's house. Silu is excited to go home and eat the clams.

When they get home, they clean the clams and put them in a big pot to boil.

28

Soon they are ready to eat.

"Niam!" says Silu. "Thanks for teaching me how to dig for clams, Anaanatsiaq. I can't wait to go clam digging again!"

Inuktitut Glossary

Notes on Inuktitut pronunciation: There are some sounds in Inuktitut that may be unfamiliar to English speakers. The pronunciations below convey those sounds in the following ways:

- A double vowel (for example, *aa, ee*) creates a long vowel sound.
- Capitalized letters indicate the emphasis.
- **q** is a "uvular" sound, which is a sound that comes from the very back of the throat (the uvula). This is different from the **k** sound, which is the same as the typical English **k** sound.

anaanatsiaq
a-NAA-nat-si-aq

grandmother

niam
NI-am

yummy

For more Inuktitut pronunciation resources, please visit inhabiteducation.com/inuitnipingit.

Nunavummi
Reading Series

The Nunavummi reading series is a Nunavut-developed levelled book series that supports literacy development while teaching readers about the people, traditions, and environment of the Canadian Arctic.

Level 9
- 16–32 pages
- Longer, more complex sentences
- Varied punctuation
- Dialogue is included in fiction texts
- Supportive images, but more information now coming from the text

10
- 16–32 pages
- Sentences and stories become longer and more complex
- Varied punctuation
- Dialogue is included in fiction texts
- Readers rely more on the words than the images to decode the text

Level 11
- 24–32 pages
- Sentences become complex and varied
- Varied punctuation
- Dialogue is included in fiction texts and is necessary to understand the story
- Readers rely more on the words than the images to decode the text

Fountas & Pinnell Text Level: K

This book has been officially levelled using the F&P Text Level Gradient™ Leveling System.